the WEATHER · DRAGONS ·

in 'Accidental Rainbows'

the WEATHER DRAGONS

in 'Accidental Rainbows'

by Wally Felts

Throw a Snowball!

Wally Felts.

Snogwash
Snow Dragon

Snubble
Sun Dragon

Slerch
Sleet Dragon

Huratio
Tornado Dragon

Ramity
Rain Dragon

Spartin
Lightning Dragon

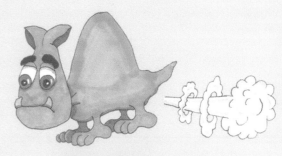

Tunder
Thunder Dragon

Frob
Frost Dragon

Clodswell
Cloud Dragon

Dripnall
Drizzle Dragon

Wingle
Wind Dragon

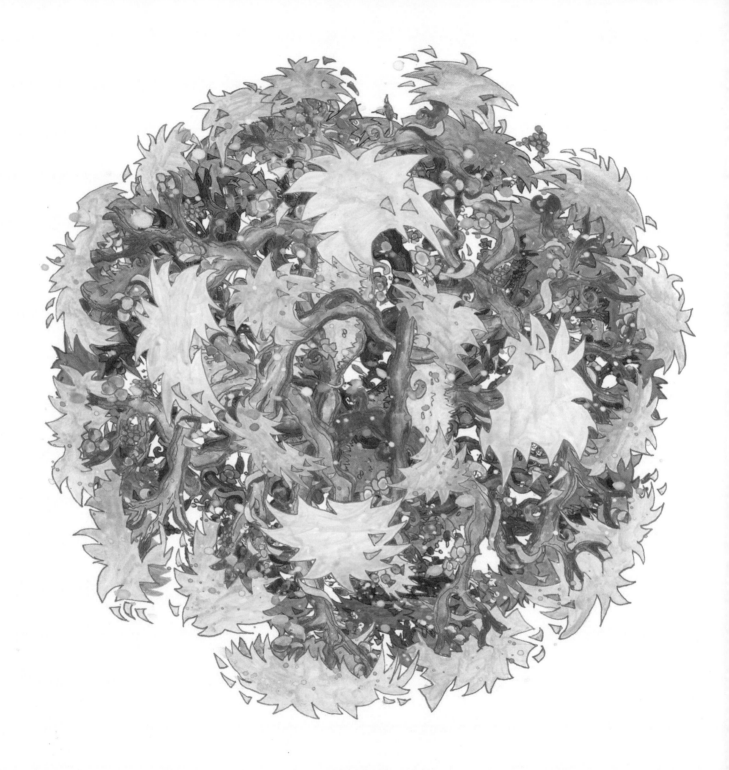

A world away in a long forgotten sky, out of sight and out of mind, drifts Fable Forest. The trees and branches twist together in and out, round and round, making the forest a giant ball of string in the sky.

Amongst the twisting trees and tangled branches, and beneath the leaves scattered like paint splattered green, live the Weather Dragons. They spice up the seasons and pepper the forest with rain, wind, sun, snow, sleet and cloud.

Whatever the weather, whenever the weather, whichever the Weather Dragon.

Way up high in the chilly prickly air, Ramity flips and flaps and flies like a bat as she spits out rain that showers the trees below. Above her buzzes Clodswell, whisking up clouds from the air with the fast beating of her tiny powerful wings.

"Bored, bored, bored!" Ramity hisses through gritted teeth.

"Rain and clouds, clouds and rain. There never is one without the other! I'm sooooooo boooored!" she whines.

Clodswell rolls her eyes and sighs. She's tired of Ramity whining and complaining. Clodswell is never cranky; she is always quiet and usually happy.

"Every dragon has their place and purpose," she whispers softly, hoping Ramity would agree. But as usual Ramity finds it easy to ignore her.

"Your clouds are just quiet, dull and grey!" Ramity declares. "And I am bored of cloudy and rainy weather." She flies off as fast as she can, leaving timid Clodswell alone in her clouds.

A small while away, quietly and calmly, Snubble is making a hidden corner of the forest sunny. He blows out sunbeams from the tip of his snout so that way down below the flowers can open their petals and come out.

It's warm and sunny and everything is happy, until out of the blue shoots a bright blue blur, flying too quickly and not giving a care.

"Look out!" cries Ramity.

"Wh-wh-what? Bu-bu-but?" splutters a very surprised Snubble.

Amongst the twists and tangles of the trees, the two dragons collide with a thundering thump which sounds like one of Tunder's short trumps.

Raindrops and sunbeams tumble and jumble, exploding into a river of colour that cascades across the sky in radiant red, organic orange, yummy yellow, gleaming green, brilliant blue, incredible indigo, vibrant violet.

The accidental rainbow shines over Fable Forest and from every knotted tree, through every twisted branch, all of the dragons can see it.

The rainbow stretches out its crystal colours like a multicoloured highway floating through the air. From here and there and everywhere, dragons pop out of hovels and hop out of holes. They climb onto boughs and balance on branches and, for the briefest of moments, the Weather Dragons stop making their weather. They all stare in wonder and fascination at the sight soaring above them.

But the colour in the sky doesn't last very long as Clodswell quickly slides down the rainbow, covering it with a plump blanket of lumpy cloud. She tries to explain with a whimper that rainbows are great but they don't make trees bigger. "Rain and sunshine don't go together. It doesn't make sense and it's not proper weather!" But her voice is so timid she can barely be heard, especially by dragons who aren't listening to her.

"Don't be ridiculous!" splutters Ramity angrily. "You are spoiling our fun and just being grumpy!"

"Let's go and get away from her!" Snubble bubbles, and off they go to make rainbows elsewhere.

Over the way and under the rainbow Snogwash is snowing and Frob is frosting. The rainbow they saw gives them each an idea: to make the sky glimmer and gleam once more.

"I could build my very own rainbow!" burbles Snogwash whilst sneezing snow out of his snout. He thinks to himself that he could start by collecting red growing fruits.

But he doesn't know that little Frob has also had a thought, which snowballs like a snowball into an idea.

"I could build my own rainbow!" squeaks small Frob, weaving tiny little webs of frost. She sees orange roots growing from the trees and knows that is one of the colours she'll need.

Spartin spits lighting across the forest sky making Tunder, as always, jump in surprise. The shock of the sharp bright light always gives Tunder a startling fright, so he jumps with a scare and lets out a loud bottom burp.

Spartin sizzles with a great new idea. "I could build my very own rainbow somewhere!" He sparks as he sees yellow petals below, and he knows that yellow is found in a rainbow.

Now at the same time, Tunder is grumbling. "I could build my own rainbow!" he thinks while still trumpeting. Without knowing Spartin was thinking the same thing, Tunder decides to scoop up the leaves that are growing and green.

Wingle blows up like a beach ball and bellows out wind, deflating like a balloon with a whispy whistle, watching the trees sway about as they rustle. She doesn't know that she isn't alone in her idea to build a rainbow of her own. "I could build my own rainbow!" she puffs and whooshes, and decides to start collecting the blue cherries that grow in the bushes.

Huratio spins in with the same idea too, but is sure that his own rainbow would withstand a tornado. He huffs and he howls as he spins on his wings, "My rainbow will be brighter than everything!" Huratio begins to blow, as he picks all the indigo berries below.

Dripnall, as usual, drips with drizzle, sitting on a tree tuft sniffling a sniffle. He has an idea to build his own rainbow, not knowing that the other dragons are doing the same thing too. "I will collect up the nuts because they are all coloured violet," sniffs Dripnall and dribbles.

When out from her tuft Slerch bounds over, all snickers and sniggles, spraying out sleet as she laughs and she giggles. Having had an idea to build a rainbow as well she exclaims, "I will pile up the seeds because they are violet as well!" She lets out a burp followed by a wet raspberry, "Blrrtthp!"

Clodswell's small voice still can't be heard as she tries to stop Snogwash and Frob from picking and digging. It's completely ignored when she says no to Spartin and Tunder who are plucking and collecting. It isn't listened to when she begs Wingle and Huratio to stop what they're doing. Slerch and Dripnall don't even notice at all when she tries to stop them gathering up the nuts and seeds with her cries and her pleads.

"The forest's natural beauty is beauty enough," Clodswell tried to protest, "Real beauty is not copied or fake, it's not something you can replicate!"

But her voice isn't loud enough to be heard amongst other voices putting themselves first.

When the dragons begin to gather other colours for their rainbows, they each find that those fruits and berries have already been picked, plucked, and ploughed by someone else.

"Give me the violet seeds," squeaks Frob frostily.

"Give me the blue cherries," squelches Slerch sleetishly.

"Give me the yellow petals," huffs Huratio huffing.

Wingle puffs up angrily, Spartin spits lightning and Tunder's bottom booms.

"I want my own rainbow!" shouts Snogwash.

"So do I!" dribbles Dripnall.

"Give me!" they all shout at each other.

"No!" they all shout back.

Lighting muddles with snow, thunder with drizzle and frost tumbles in the wind, the weather is all over everything.

The fruit fight that follows is a full on, splodgy mishmash of hurling berries and flying fruits. Splat go the berries, splodge go the cherries, and squelch go the other fruits. Yellow guck is flung through the air with indigo smush sticking everywhere. The forest quickly becomes a sticky, mushy mess of thick, gluey jam, and the dragons are splattered with the mucky rainbow marmalade. The dragons chuckle and chuck everything and anything they can get their paws on, when suddenly...

A loud slap echoes through the trees as a ripe, red, bulbous fruit hits Clodswell smack on her head. The fruit fight stops as quickly as it started, and the dragons stand frozen in regret.

Clodswell hovers silently for a second as thick sticky red fruit juice drips down her cheek, muddled with a solitary tear.

The dragons had not listened to her since they began building their fake rainbows and Clodswell can speak softly no longer.

"Look what you have done!" Clodswell roars in her loudest of loud voices. She points to the forest that had been picked, cut, hacked, chopped, dug, sploshed, squashed, and squelched.

"The trees are lifeless and bare. There are no more red fruits, orange roots, yellow petals, green leaves, blue cherries, indigo berries or violet seeds!" Clodswell splutters. The other dragons are stunned and astounded. They've never, ever heard Clodswell speak so sternly. They know she is right, for as they look around they see that Fable Forest is faded and desolate. The branches are crying, the bark is sorry and the trees are sad.

The dragons see what is right because nothing is left.

"We are so very sorry," squeaks Frob.

"If only we had listened," sneezes Snogwash.

"We didn't mean to make you angry," sizzles Spartin.

Clodswell, meanwhile, is confident that she knows what to do. She hands them all buckets and mops to clean up the mess and fix what they broke. Then she quickly flies off, leaving them in the bubbles. For the forest to grow, she needs Ramity and Snubble.

Clodswell fetches Ramity and Snubble and shows them the trees that hang limply and troubled. There are no berries or cherries or roots or fruits.

Ramity and Snubble do what they're told, because Clodswell is confident, firm, clear, and bold. Snubble is sent to blow sunbeams on cherries and berries and flowers and fruits, so they will ripen and open and grow like they should.

Ramity sprinkles her rain on the roots and seeds, and the nuts and the leaves. She is happy seeing Clodswell hovering above her. Cloudy and rainy, for Ramity, is how it's supposed to be.

With rain over here and shine over there, the forest is growing back everywhere. In no time it fills with fruits, flowers, cherries, and berries, all the colours of the rainbow.

But deep down in the dragons' hearts, they really do miss the beauty of the real rainbow. So every so often and on some occasions, Clodswell gives a treat to all of the dragons. She allows Ramity and Snubble to mix raindrops and sunbeams to create beautiful rainbows that fly high in the sky for all to admire.

And when playtime is over, Clodswell uses her clouds to cover over the rainbow and the dragons know to start making their weather.

Whatever the weather, whenever the weather, whichever the Weather Dragon.

Wally Felts

Paul 'Wally' Felts studied film theory and animation before teacher training and was Assistant Head Teacher in an outstanding South London primary school. A lead practitioner for the British Film Institute's Media Literacy program, he was awarded Senior Associate status at the Teaching and Learning Academy and is a Specialist Schools and Academies Trust scholar.

Wally has written and independently produced original school musical productions and runs animation workshops for children of all ages. He lives in Vancouver with his wife and two daughters.

Copyright

Produced by:

FriesenPress
Suite 300 – 852 Fort Street
Victoria, BC, Canada V8W 1H8

www.friesenpress.com

Distributed to the trade by The Ingram Book Company

CPSIA information can be obtained
at www.ICGtesting.com
Printed in the USA
LVIC06n2344120514
385464LV00001B/1

* 9 7 8 1 4 6 0 2 3 9 0 9 4 *